DINOSAURS:
Giant Jigsaws

By Jo Windsor

Contents

Rigby

DINOSAURS:

Giant Jigsaws

Scientists spend hours studying and rebuilding dinosaur skeletons so that they can find out about the animals that lived and died millions of years ago. When the reconstruction is complete, scientists are more able to understand:

– how the animal moved

– whether it walked on two or four legs

– whether it was a meat-eater or a plant-eater

when reconstruction is complete

Digging Up a Dinosaur

PREDICT...

What information do you think you will find in this chapter?

Dinosaur *digs* are carried out in many parts of the world. Everything that is known about dinosaurs has come from what the experts have discovered through their findings at these digs.

At a dig, great care is taken to remove the bones from the ground or rock without damaging them. Hammers, chisels, and even dentist drills are used to chip away the material that holds the bones. Soft brushes are used to clean away earth and stone. Bones that might crumble are painted with special glues to harden them and hold them together.

experts have discovered

Photographs are taken of the dig to show the position of the bones lying in the ground. By studying the pictures and looking at the surroundings, the palaeontologist is more able to understand how the animal lived and died.

Before being transported to a laboratory, the bones are wrapped in tissue paper for protection, then in plaster-soaked bandages or special foam jackets that harden. The palaeontologist writes a report numbering all the pieces of bone and describing their condition. This will help in the reconstruction of the dinosaur skeleton.

Clarify ?

palaeontologist

a doctor

b a person who moves skeletons

c a person who studies fossils
to find out about extinct
animals and plants

A, B or C?

In the Laboratory

PREDICT....

What information do you think you will find in this chapter?

Before a dinosaur skeleton can be rebuilt, the bones must be carefully checked, cleaned, and preserved. Bone is hard, so when an animal dies, the flesh rots away and the bones remain. After a long time, they turn into a kind of rock called fossilized bone.

Around the fossilized bone is hard rock that is called the matrix. It may have become stuck to the bone over many millions of years and must be cleared away. It is a very delicate job.

Scientists use special equipment to help complete this job carefully.

The special tools that scientists use include:

- microscopes to check the fossilized bones
- brushes to clean away pieces of dust from the surface of bones
- an air blaster to take off tiny pieces of rock without damaging the bones underneath
- a pneumatic pen, like a mini road drill, to break away the rock
- special glue to stop the rock from breaking (any gaps in the rock can also be filled to make sure the fossil does not fall apart)
- vats of acid to dissolve away the matrix from the bone (protective clothing must always be worn when lowering the bones and rock into the vat)
- vacuum systems to suck up fine dust

What questions might be asked about the safety of people working with these tools?

Reconstructing the Skeleton

PREDICT...

What information do you think you will find in this chapter?

Scientists work very hard to reconstruct a dinosaur's skeleton in a natural position, so that it will look as it did millions of years ago. They need to know how the skeletons of living animals are constructed and how they function. Studying today's animals gives important clues as to how dinosaurs' bodies worked.

skeletons of the living

When a dinosaur's bones are found, they are usually not complete. Often, bones from the skeleton are missing or badly damaged. Replacement bones are sometimes made out of fiberglass (a reinforced plastic material) and used to complete the skeleton.

All the cleaned bones and those made of fiberglass are laid out in their correct order. They are carefully studied to understand how they fit together.

are usually

Question

How do you think the scientists use their knowledge to create the missing pieces of skeleton?

To hold the bones in place, an engineer makes a steel framework that will support the bones. The leg bones are put on first, then the spine, and ribs. Finally, the tail and skull are added. The skeleton is now ready to go on display in a museum.

In some museums, dinosaur skeletons are put together by hanging the bones from the museum's ceiling, using steel wires. The bones look as if they are joined, but are really hanging from the ceiling like a giant puppet.

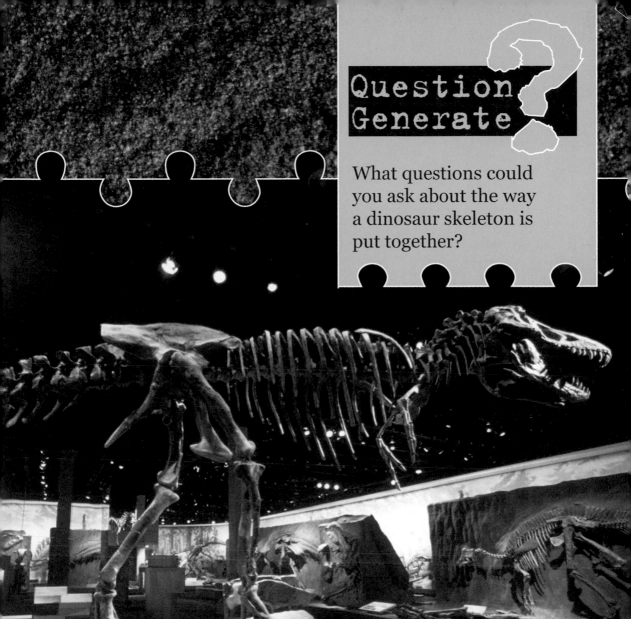

What questions could you ask about the way a dinosaur skeleton is put together?

Bringing Dinosaurs to Life

Discovering where a dinosaur's muscles were fixed to the bones of its skeleton provides an important clue as to what the dinosaur looked like. Although the muscles themselves have not survived, the marks showing where they were attached to the fossil bones can still be seen. The fossil bones display rough places, or ridges, where muscles were once attached. Scientists are able to figure out what the missing muscles must have looked like.

The muscles of the dinosaur held its bones together and gave the body its shape. Using their knowledge, scientists can tell how big the muscles were and how much flesh there was on the body.

Scientists also study the muscles of living reptiles considered to be most closely related to dinosaurs. They watch how these reptiles move, and use this as a model when recreating the way dinosaurs moved.

Artists can then work closely with the scientists to build up a picture of what the dinosaur looked like. They draw sketches or make models that show muscles, flesh, and skin added to the skeleton.

Dinosaur skin was perfectly suited for life on the land. Skin impressions that have been found in rock are usually small, because after death, an animal's skin rots away quickly. From their findings, scientists believe dinosaur skin was tough, scaly, bony, knobbly, and waterproof. No one knows for sure the color of a dinosaur or whether it had stripes or spots.

FACT

A statement that can be proved to be true.

OPINION

A view or belief that is not based on fact or knowledge.

Fact	Opinion
?	?

Find some examples!

Robotic Dinosaurs

PREDICT . . .

What information do you think you will find in this chapter?

Computer experts, designers, engineers, and palaeontologists combine their skills to make robotic dinosaurs. These robots give us information about how the creatures moved, fought, and even snarled and bared their teeth.

Robotic dinosaurs are involved structures that have metal working parts, a soundtrack of dinosaur noises, and a computer to control the movements. The body is often made out of polyurethane and foam that is easy and light to carve into a dinosaur shape. This foam is painted to look real.

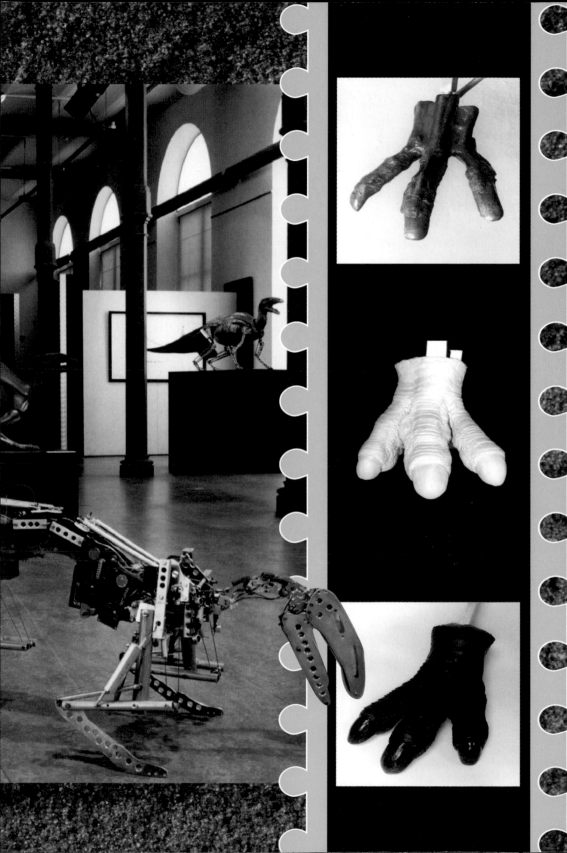

From work scientists have done reconstructing dinosaurs and building robotic dinosaurs, a great understanding has been gained about creatures that lived millions of years ago. This knowledge is also used by computer technicians when making programs that include images of dinosaurs that are used in the film industry. These images are really lifelike and add real excitement to the movies and videos that we watch!

Key Points

"Digs" are carried out in many parts of the world.

Scientists reconstruct dinosaur skeletons so they can find out about these animals.

They use special equipment to reconstruct the dinosaur skeletons.

?

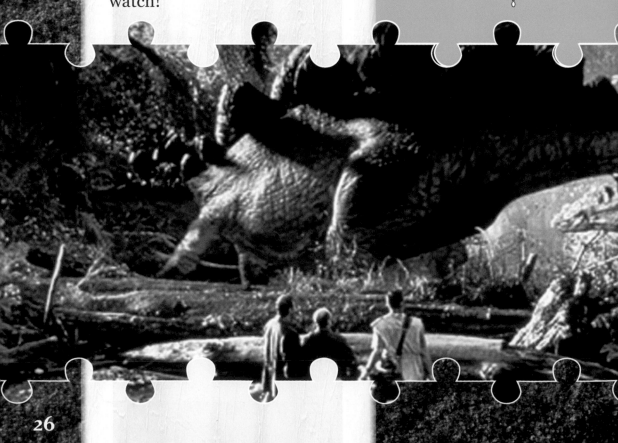

DINOSAUR

Interesting Facts

Looking at photos helps us to understand how the animal lived and died.

Bones are wrapped in tissue paper and plaster-soaked bandages.

Index

Think About the Text

Making connections –
What connections can you
make with the text?

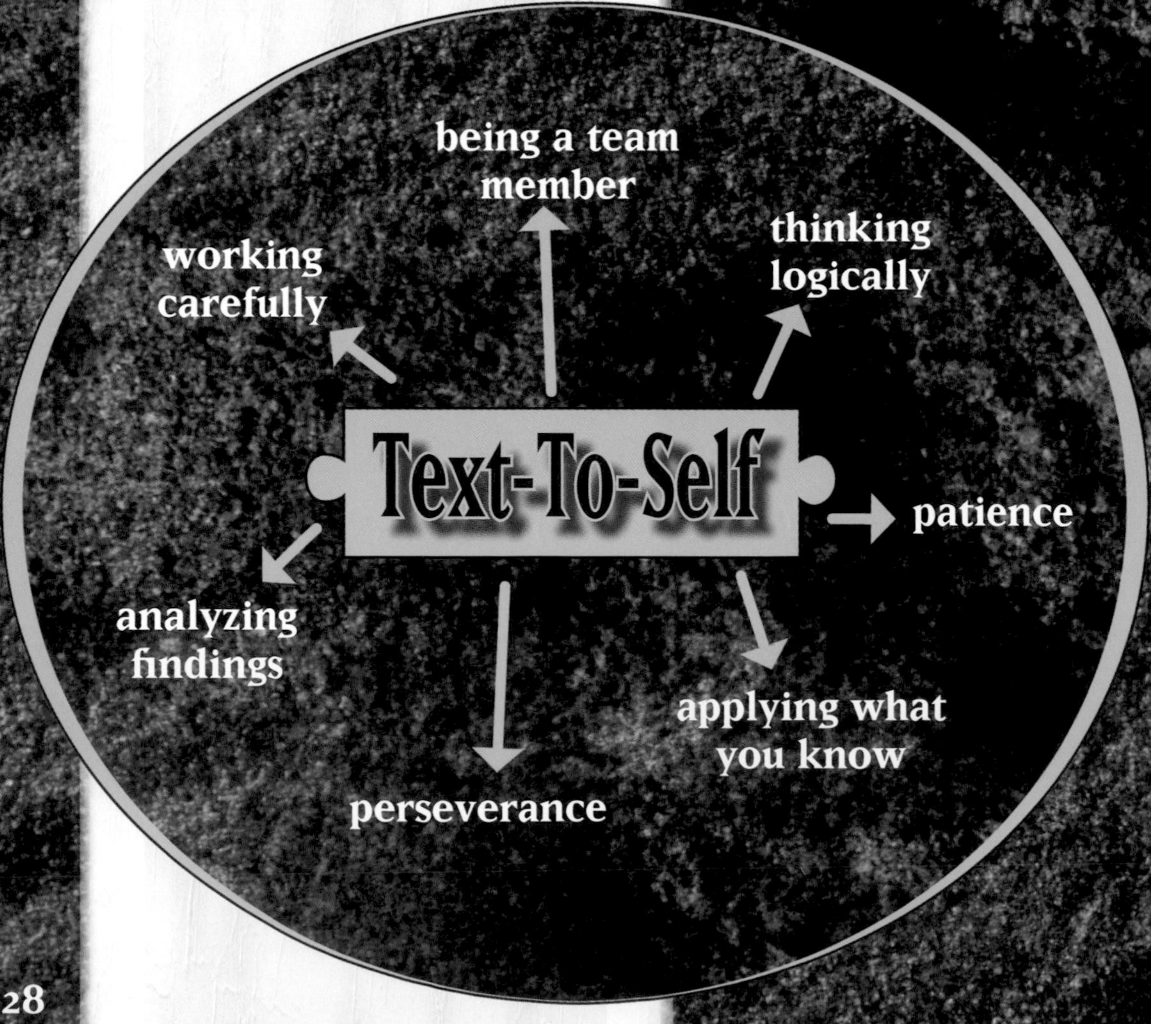

being a team
member

working
carefully

thinking
logically

Text-To-Self

patience

analyzing
findings

applying what
you know

perseverance

Text-To-Text

Talk about other informational texts you may have read that have similar features. Compare the texts.

Text-To-World

Talk about situations in the world that might connect to elements in the text.

Plannning an Informational Report

1

Organize the information

Select a topic

List the things you know and which things you need to research.

What I know:

Scientists look for evidence to find out more about dinosaurs.

Many types of dinosaurs.

People dig up the bones.

What I will research:

How dinosaur skeletons are reconstructed.

What information scientists get from the bones.

How they go about digging them up.

What happens to the bones.

2

Locate the information you will need

Library

Internet

Experts

3

Process the information

Skim read.

Sort your ideas into groups.

Make some headings.

4
Plan the report

Write a general introduction.

5
Decide on a logical order for your information

What will come first, next ... last.

6
Write up your information

7
Design some visuals to include in your report

You can use: graphs, diagrams, labels, charts, tables, cross-sections...

An Informational Report

a Records information

b Has no unnecessary descriptive details

c Has no metaphors or similes

d Uses scientific or technical terms

e Uses the present tense

f Is written in a formal style that is concise and accurate

g Has a logical sequence of facts

h Avoids author bias or opinion